and the
Mammoth

First published 2005
Evans Brothers Limited
2A Portman Mansions
Chiltern Street
London W1U 6NR

British Library Cataloguing in Publication Data

French, Vivian
        Cave-baby and the mammoth. – (Twisters)
        1. Children's stories – Pictorial works
        I. Title
        823.9'14 [J]

ISBN 0237529319
13-digit ISBN (from 1 January 2007) 9780237529314

Printed in China by WKT Company Limited

Series Editor: Nick Turpin
Design: Robert Walster
Production: Jenny Mulvanny
Series Consultant: Gill Matthews

Cave-baby and the Mammoth

Vivian French
and Lisa Williams

Evans

"Waah!" wailed Cave-baby.
"Ssh!" said Cave-dad.

"Waah!" screamed
Cave-baby.

Thump! Thump!

8

"Mammoth!" shouted Cave-dad.

9

"Run!" shouted Cave-mum.

13

THUMP! THUMP!

"WHERE'S MY BABY?"
yelled Cave-mum.

18

"Waaaaaaaaah" wailed the mammoth.

"CLEVER baby!" said
Cave-mum.
"Goo," said Cave-baby.

Why not try reading another Twisters book?

Not-so-silly Sausage by Stella Gurney and Liz Million
ISBN 0 237 52875 4

Nick's Birthday by Jane Oliver and Silvia Raga
ISBN 0 237 52896 7

Out Went Sam by Nick Turpin and Barbara Nascimbeni
ISBN 0 237 52894 0

Yummy Scrummy by Paul Harrison and Belinda Worsley
ISBN 0 237 52876 2

Squelch! by Kay Woodward and Stefania Colnaghi
ISBN 0 237 52895 9

Sally Sails the Seas by Stella Gurney and Belinda Worsley
ISBN 0 237 52893 2

Billy on the Ball by Paul Harrison and Silvia Raga
ISBN 0 237 52926 2

Countdown by Kay Woodward and Ofra Amit
ISBN 0 237 52927 0

One Wet Welly by Gill Matthews and Belinda Worsley
ISBN 0 237 52928 9

Sand Dragon by Su Swallow and Silvia Raga
ISBN 0 237 52929 7

Cave-baby and the Mammoth by Vivian French and Lisa Williams
ISBN 0 237 52931 9

Albert Liked Ladders by Su Swallow and Barbara Nascimbeni
ISBN 0 237 52930 0